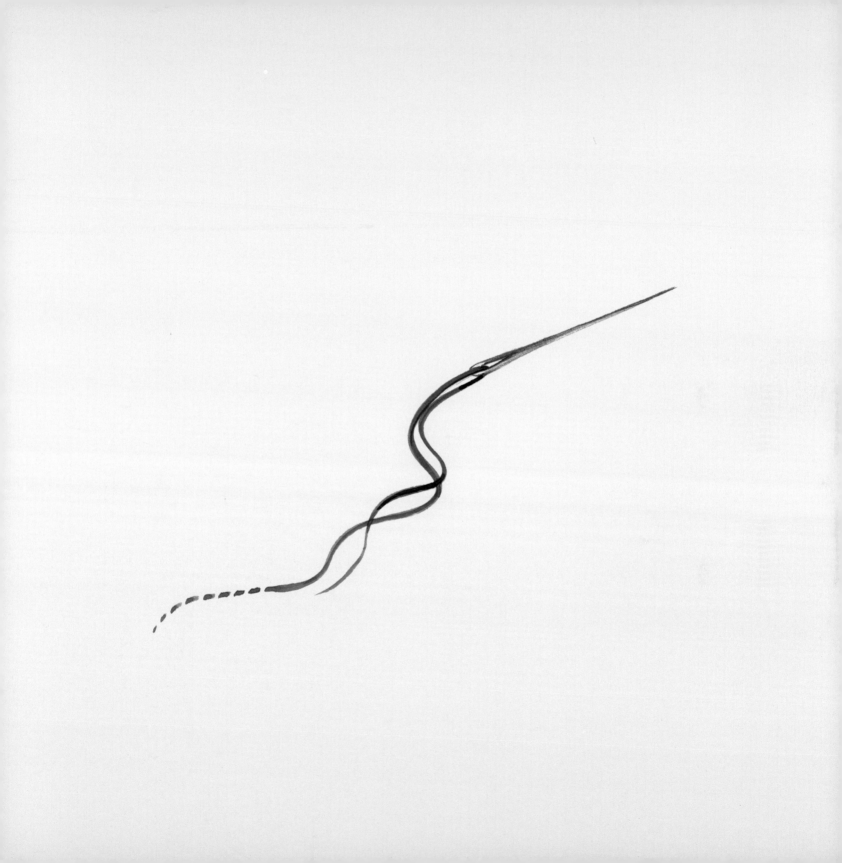

Sadiq Wants To Stitch

First U.S. Print July 2019
First Reprint India

Text: Mamta Nainy
Illustrations: Niloufer Wadia

Karadi Tales Company Pvt. Ltd.
3A Dev Regency, 11 First Main Road,
Gandhi Nagar, Adyar, Chennai 600020
Tel: +91-44-42054243
email: contact@karaditales.com
Website: www.karaditales.com

ISBN: 978-81-9338-891-4

Distributed in the United States by Consortium Book Sales & Distribution
www.cbsd.com

Cataloging - in - Publication information:
Nainy, Mamta
Sadiq Wants to Stitch / Mamta Nainy; illustrated by Niloufer Wadia
p.36; color illustrations; 24.5 x 24 cm.

JUV000000 JUVENILE FICTION / General
JUV039000 JUVENILE FICTION / Social Themes
JUV005000 JUVENILE FICTION / Boys & Men
JUV013000 JUVENILE FICTION / Family / General
JUV030020 JUVENILE FICTION / People & Places / Asia
JUV074000 JUVENILE FICTION / Diversity & Multicultural

Sadiq wants to stitch

Mamta Nainy

Niloufer Wadia

Sadiq woke up to the soft gurgling sound of the river Lidder. At this early hour, it was the only sound that filled the valley.

He slipped out from under his thin quilt into the chill of the dawn. Ammi was already awake, and busy preparing his midday meal. Sadiq had a quick wash, offered namaz, and sipped his noon-cha.

He was now ready to milk the sheep and then take them to the meadows – a chore he had inherited after Abba's death two years ago.

Sadiq walked across the hilltops with his flock in tow.

He thought of the approaching winter and how he and the other members of his community would move southwards before the river became, as Ammi would often say, a herd of wild bulls rising from their sleep.

While the sheep grazed, Sadiq studied the tinge of yellow on the beak of a magpie.

It was the same color that Ammi had used in her stitches on one of her rugs. In Sadiq's eyes, Ammi made the most beautiful embroidered rugs in the whole of Kashmir!

Sadiq too loved to embroider. He was happiest when his long needle danced through a maze of multi-colored threads and wondrous patterns came alive under his fingers.

Ammi sometimes guided him on how to move his fingers to get the stitches nice and neat. However, Sadiq could tell that she wasn't too happy when he stitched.

After the sheep had grazed,
Sadiq led his flock to his tent.
Inside, he saw Ammi look up
from her work and smile at him.

Spread across the floor, in front
of her, was a beautiful woven rug.

"Because, in our community, it is the women who stitch. Men tend to the sheep," said Ammi, without taking her eyes off the needle that went deftly in and out of the rug. "Have you ever seen any other boy in our community stitch?"

"No, but..." started Sadiq.

Ammi cut off Sadiq before he could continue with his protests. "You do your work and let me do mine. Now go and get some firewood for cooking," she insisted.

That night, Sadiq had a dream. There were colorful threads all around him. He went from one to the other, bringing the threads together in a rich floral design on a rug.

Ammi looked at his embroidered rug and gave him a hug.

Sadiq opened his eyes. He lifted his tousled head from his pillow and decided that he would stitch.

Every night after that, when Ammi
fell asleep, Sadiq tiptoed to a corner.

In the stillness of the night, his fingers
worked on a rug like fluttering butterflies
on the grass.

On the last day of the week,
Sadiq woke up and found Ammi
still in bed with a high fever.

"Ah, what fate!" said Ammi,
trying to get up. "What will I tell
Abdul Chacha when he comes this
evening? I haven't started on
the second rug yet."

"Don't worry, Ammi," said Sadiq,
offering her a cup of noon-cha.
"We will see what to do when
he comes."

That evening, when Abdul Chacha came to collect the embroidered rugs, Ammi handed him the one she had completed.

"And the other one?" he asked her.

Ammi started to explain.
"Abdul bhai, I wasn't able to..."

"I have it with me," said Sadiq,
before Ammi could finish
her sentence.

He pulled out a rug from
underneath his mattress.

Abdul Chacha looked at the rug.
"This is lovely!" he exclaimed.
"But isn't this different from
what I ordered?" he asked.

Ammi was beside herself with disbelief.

"You made this?" she asked Sadiq, who quietly nodded.

She took the rug from Abdul Chacha and ran her fingers lightly over it.

"I would like to keep this," she said.

"Please give me a few more days. Now that I have my little boy to help, I'll have your second rug ready in no time!" she told him, beaming.

Abdul Chacha agreed and patted Sadiq.

Ammi then wrapped her arms around Sadiq and gave him a tight hug, just as he had dreamt the other night.

"So you want to stitch, eh? Don't think it is easy. I am going to work you very hard. And no neglecting your other chores."

The next morning, much to Sadiq's delight, Ammi displayed his rug for everyone to see. And when people gathered around to admire its patterns, Ammi told them, her voice bursting with pride, that it was her son Sadiq who had embroidered it.

THE BAKARWALS OF KASHMIR

The Bakarwals are a nomadic community of shepherds and goatherds in the Pir Panjal ranges and the Himalayan Mountains of Jammu and Kashmir in India. The word 'Bakarwal' means 'people who take care of goats and sheep'.

The community travels to the verdant areas of the Kashmir valley to escape the heat of Jammu, and with the onset of winter, the tribe slowly makes its way to warmer regions. Their journey is long and hard, and they often brave rough weather. Noon-cha, a tea made with milk, salt and baking powder, is a popular beverage among the people here to keep them warm in the winter.

Bakarwal men tend, feed, and guard flocks of sheep and goats, and earn their livelihood by trading wool. The women of the community are known for their unique embroidery skills.

They create embroidered pouches, clutches, saddle cloth, wall-hangings, slings, bags, and more. It is said that Bakarwal women choose colors according to their moods. Like other shepherd crafts, Bakarwal embroidery is slowly dying out and there is an urgent need to revive it.

Mamta Nainy spent some years in advertising before a rotten apple fell on her head while she was sitting under a mango tree, and she had her Eureka moment. Now all she does is write for children, devour books and cupcakes, play with a yo-yo, and write some more. She lives and dreams in Delhi.

Niloufer Wadia quit her 20-year career in advertising to follow her passion - illustration and painting. She works in traditional and digital media. Storybook illustration happened quite by chance, but this is her seventh picture book and while it has gone well so far, she believes she has miles to go, and much to learn.